Casual Encounters

WITH WOMEN
FROM WORK

ANDRÉ BRISCOE

ISBN: 979-8-9896369-1-4

Published by Azarel Publishing

Edited by Shawna Brim

Cover design by Israr Khan and Anaya Khan

This novel is a work of fiction.

Names, characters, organizations, places, events, and incidents are either products of the author's imagination or are used fictitiously.

Prologue

"Speak of the devil and the motherfucker appears."

That was the way Cleon, my best friend since grade school, acknowledged me when I entered his barbershop. His peculiar way of greeting me only meant that my personal business was today's hot topic. You see, Cleon was not just the owner of Goodfellas Barbershop, he also made it his priority to be its resident entertainer.

Let him tell it, he knew everything about everybody. Even if he didn't know, Cleon was such a colorful storyteller that it was always a good time listening to whatever came out of his mouth. Goodfellas Barbershop, like any Black barbershop, was a place that brothers visited for the camaraderie just as much as they came to get a haircut – sometimes we could come through just for the good vibes.

"I was just lecturing these amateurs on why you don't get involved with women at the workplace. You got the night club. The gym. There's Walmart. Even church is fair game. But this fool right here messes up his money spot over what I'm sure was just a few minutes of pleasure."

Cleon had the entire barbershop audience laughing and applauding at my expense. I didn't appreciate Cleon using my real-life drama to amuse everyone, but honestly, I'd be all in on the fun if it was someone else that he was ragging on. Besides, he was only sharing details that were public record. All anyone had to do was watch the local news or google it. I stood there, fake laughing with everyone, but neither Cleon nor anyone else in attendance knew how much emotional distress I was carrying around.

What went down shouldn't happen to any person, and especially not at their place of employment, but I was finding out that living to talk about it was both a blessing and a curse. I was relieved that I survived. It was just difficult to live with the fact that because of my selfish actions, someone else no longer was.

"All I want to know is was the box worth the trouble?"

The laughter died down, and all eyes were on me. From the moment I stepped in the door, he was clowning me so hard that the only way to respond was to hit him with a joke of my own. I needed to be quick about it because taking too long would have everyone thinking Cleon got the best of me.

"You'd know it was worth it if you actually got some to talk about."

The shop erupted in laughter at my clap back. Cleon couldn't get in a retaliation with all the commotion and high fives going on. Now, everyone was ragging on him and the long-standing joke that his game was weak when it came to the ladies.

"Man, fuck what y'all talking about," refuted Cleon.

He smacked his lips and waved off the celebrations, never liking the taste of defeat at his own game. Without others noticing, I winked at Cleon as a way to let him know I won the round. He nodded, agreeing that I got one on him.

"But all jokes aside, is everything good with you?" Cleon changed his tone to serious concern.

"Yeah, bro. I'm good," I lied.

"So, Brands, what really went down?"

Darius, one of the barbers, inquired from the other end of the shop while touching up the hairline of a customer sitting in his chair. I could sense the compassion for my well-being, not just asking to be nosey or to further make a mockery out of the situation like Cleon was.

"Don't let this clown speak your gospel. You know damn well he's a false prophet."

Cleon threw up a middle finger at Darius. He was right though. Everybody knew Cleon was a know-it-all who habitually got the facts wrong more times than he was ever right. If I didn't make it a point to tell my side of the story, Cleon's version would be the only one his shop's patrons would come to know. There was no way in hell that I would allow this chapter of my story to be forever penned by the likes of Cleon.

I scanned the room from left to right. The men in attendance weren't my blood relatives, but I connected with them like they were my brothers, cousins, uncles, and father figures. I'd have a difficult time sitting in a confessional and sharing my wrongdoings with a priest, but spilling my guts to my barbershop family was just another day in the hood. I took a deep breath, cleared my throat, and decided I was ready to sit in the hot seat.

"So, what had happened was..."

Chapter 1

I was seated at the guest side of my manager's desk, pretending to pay attention. I tried but couldn't focus on what she was saying with what was protruding from her blouse. Since the start of our meeting, her face was directed into a sales report, so she had no idea I was checking her out until she briefly glanced up. I was so stuck on stupid that I didn't even notice she had caught me with my eyes locked on her chest.

"So, Mr. Brandston, care to explain these numbers or do you intend to just sit there and stare at my breasts?"

"Temporary setback. Nothing I can't immediately improve," I quickly and plainly responded with my eyes still fixed on her chest region.

Last month's poor work performance was past tense as far as I was concerned. Providing an excuse wouldn't solve anything, and right now, I was more interested in addressing her second question in greater detail.

"And yes, I do."

"You do what?" she inquired.

"I see something I like, and so I'll keep looking."

I felt suave and cocky in my approach. I took my shot, and I was happy that I did. I'd been torturing myself for the last three years, seeing her every day and not crossing the line. Now that it was over with Evette – our toxic five-year relationship ended last month – this was my chance to get back on the bull.

"Mr. Brandston–"

"Actually, if you don't mind, everyone around the office and all my loved ones calls me Brands," I interjected, wanting to remove the formalities, so we could ease into some personal chitchat.

She sat back in her chair, crossed her arms and let out a long sigh before responding as if she was choosing her next words wisely. Internally, I knew I had just messed up. At any given second, her alter ego – Angry Black Woman – was about to pay me a visit I wasn't prepared for.

"When the day comes that someone else in this office takes over the responsibilities of signing your check, I'll call you whatever you'd like. Until then, Mr. Brandston, how about we keep this company's professional expectations in mind?" She added some human resources seriousness to her tone.

"Yes, ma'am!" I asserted my understanding, taking the hint to quit while I was ahead.

There were a few seconds of silence that felt much longer. I was so nervous my underarms were itchy. Only other human being to put me in my place like that was my momma. Right now, I was more scared of my boss than I ever was of the woman who for eighteen years tirelessly tried beating the black off of me.

"You've been number one in sales for all the years you have been on my team. How you ended up dead last just doesn't make any sense to me. I'll go along with this being a temporary setback if you can assure me that's all it was."

"Won't happen again," I said with confidence.

"Good, then we're done here. Please close the door behind you."

I dashed for the door, pausing just as I was turning the knob. I felt the need to redeem myself for flirting earlier. I didn't want her to think I was *that guy*. She noticed my hesitation to exit and seemed annoyed.

"What is it, Mr. Brandston?"

"Well, I just wanted to apologize."

"There's no need for apologies. I've had my fair share of bad numbers when I was in your shoes. It happens to the best of us."

"Not for that. Look, I was out of line, and I fully understand if you have to report it. I just want you to know that I'm sorry if I offended you in any way," I said humbly.

"Thank you for saying that. Honestly, the only issue was you failed to utilize my golden rule in our line of business."

Properly learn your audience. I'd heard that a million times. That was her most used phrase at every morning sales huddle whenever a deal wasn't closed. Anytime a salesperson had an excuse as to why they couldn't get the job done, she would always say, "*If I don't know who I am selling to, I can't convince them to buy a damn thing.*"

"Now think about rule number two on your way out," she said in a dismissive way.

Heading back to my desk, I grinned from ear-to-ear as if I was a ten-year-old who'd just ripped the wrapping paper off the one gift I was hoping to receive for Christmas. I knew all this time she wanted me, probably even more than I wanted her. There wasn't a woman in the world who could resist six-foot-three, two-twenty, with a bald head, and a size thirteen shoe. My manhood was restored from the beatdown I took in her office.

Rule number two. *If at first you don't succeed, try again until you do.*

Chapter 2

Sherie was relaxed in her office chair and spoke freely. This was a more pleasant visit than last month. My sales numbers were back at the top where they belonged, and I felt confident enough to strike a conversation about something other than business. I could sense she needed to take her mind off of the work grind. Noticing the graduate degree hanging on the wall behind her, I changed our discussion about sales quotas and got her talking about her alma mater.

She spoke proudly about the education she received from Western Governors University, about her history with the company, how she was promoted to management so quickly, and what struggles she had to endure being the only Black and woman manager in the entire southwest region. Then we switched from company business to her entertaining me with stories about growing up around the crazy ass Puerto Ricans she had to endure in the Humboldt Park neighborhood on the west side of Chicago.

It was forty-five minutes past our meeting time. We easily could've enjoyed each other's company the rest of the workday, but a buzzing iPhone on the desk alerted that her next appointment would begin in fifteen minutes. Realizing that the reason for my office visit was not complete, she checked her calendar for the next available time we could get together to finalize my monthly performance review.

Since this friendly exchange worked out better than expected, I asked what she thought about discussing it after work over some drinks or dinner. Sherie stopped scrolling through her smartphone's calendar and gave me an ear-to-ear smile, apparently in love with the idea. It only took a second for her to realize that her reaction exposed way too much excitement about going on a dinner date with a subordinate. She forced her face back into her phone and with a corporate tone agreed to meet me at five o'clock.

Sherie walked with me to my cubicle to chat further about our evening plans. We used a lot of head nods and hand gestures so that prying eyes would assume we were in deep discussion about something work related. In reality, we were deciding on what to eat and where. She liked my suggestion of soul food at Mrs. White's Golden Rule Café in downtown Phoenix.

I couldn't help but fixate over Sherie as she walked back to her office. She wore black slacks that tightly hugged her thighs, hips, and backside. She owned an apple bottom that looked too damn good to be true, and the slacks were so fitting that I could tell she was either wearing thong panties or none at all. Every step she took in her heels made that booty gyrate and even more enticing to stare at.

I couldn't get back to focusing on work the rest of my shift. My mind was too busy wondering what I needed to say to get closer to Sherie, and what it would take to get her fine ass out of those slacks.

Chapter 3

Mrs. White's café was small yet cozy and stayed packed because it was the best soul food spot in town. We had to park our cars about a half of block from the restaurant. This gave Sherie time to make small talk; however, I was too busy checking out her amazing body to keep up with the conversation. I was thankful that the sidewalk was narrow, leaving me no choice but to be a gentleman and let the lady walk in front of me as we headed for the entrance of the restaurant. She knew what I was up to behind her, but not once did she mention any objection.

Even though this get together was work related, I felt like Sherie was dressed as if we were officially off-the-clock. She changed out of the business attire she had on earlier into more of a casual date ensemble; one that made the hell-like June temperatures in Phoenix more bearable, and also the type of outfit that ensured her male companion had all the eye candy he needed for the evening.

From head to toe, Sherie possessed a remarkable sense of fashion. Barely covering her five-foot-five package was an emerald green strapless romper. She decorated her look with rose cut diamond earrings, a gold herringbone choker necklace, Pandora bracelet with multiple charms on her left wrist, Gucci wallet clutched in her right hand, and these extremely sexy purple heels that laced up her calves. Her uncovered skin was shiny and smooth, like she bathed in holy water then lathered every inch of her body with baby oil. Damn, she was stunning!

She cleared her throat excessively to snap me out of the hypnosis her beauty had me under. Sherie paused at the entrance of the restaurant, hinting that she knew my mother raised me better. I rushed to open the door and apologized for forgetting my manners. Before following her inside, I made sure to take another long look at that badonkadonk that bounced in after her.

Once seated, we were both more concerned with staring at each other and talking it up than ordering food, asking several times for the impatient waitress to give us a few more minutes. Our conversation was all over the place and flowed naturally. We chatted like best friends about the last movie we'd seen in theaters, our favorite vacation spots, if Suge and Puffy had anything to do with killing Tupac and Biggie, and how we would spend a million dollars. She lost some cool points when she revealed that she was a Pittsburgh Steelers fan – division rivals to my Baltimore Ravens – and that she voted twice for Hillary Clinton only because she was a woman, not because she was a better candidate than Barack Obama or Donald Trump.

Several times throughout the date, I found myself having internal self-talks about how she was everything I desired in a woman. I knew it was only the first day of getting to know her outside of the office, but everything about her felt so genuine. Sherie was more than the pretty face, slim waist, thick thighs, and big butt that I usually went for. On top of having all those physical features, she was intelligent, goal-driven, attentive, and didn't make me feel uncomfortable about being my boss. Only thing left to confirm was that she was a freak in the sheets and could cook like momma – then I'd know for sure she was a keeper.

We were having so much fun that before we knew it, two hours had passed. We barely ate but did have a few drinks. We kept each other laughing and googly-eyed one another the whole time. Once again, we failed to complete the main reason for this get together. Sherie requested that we were serious long enough to conduct company business and began sharing her grade of my work performance for the month.

Honestly, I couldn't focus on anything she was saying because I was visualizing what it would feel like to suck on that hard, rather large, nipple poking through her silk top. It wasn't at all cold in the restaurant, so I assumed it was entirely my fault that I was being treated to the mouthwatering image. She giggled and lightly tapped me when she realized that once again, I was unable to provide any feedback because my eyes were obsessed with her chest region. I was probably out of line, her being my boss, but she was just too sexy not to make a move.

Just as I scooted closer in her direction, the waitress rudely dropped the check on the table and informed us that the restaurant closed an hour ago. Now aware of the time, she frantically blurted out a couple of curse words and fumbled through her purse to retrieve cash from her pocketbook. Not sure if it was because she was in a rush or it was just her norm, but she placed a hundred-dollar bill on the table. Before I could take offense for not allowing me to be the chivalrous gentleman that I was and pay the bill, she was moving quickly out of her seat and heading toward the exit.

I sat there for a moment confused by her frantic actions, then followed after her attempting to match her pace to find out why she was in such a hurry to leave. Sherie ignored me when I called her name, scrambling through her purse in search of car keys. Still cussing at herself, she was mumbling something about the terrible mistake she'd made having dinner with me.

I grabbed her left arm attempting to turn her to face me, hoping this act would convince her to give me a moment of her attention. As she jerked her arm free in a *don't-touch-me-like-that* kind of way, I noticed for the first time the enormous piece of gold on her ring finger with a ridiculously large diamond attached to it. My mouth and eyes were wide open, shocked at the sight of her jewelry that unmistakably let me know that I'd been investing quality time into a married woman.

Why had I never seen her wearing that before? It was huge! Her husband most certainly wanted any two-legged dog sniffing her way to know she was spoken for. Now the urgency made sense. It was only eight-thirty, but it would be hard for a married woman to explain why she was getting home a few hours later than normal and wasn't answering the multiple back-to-back calls and messages from her husband.

The impeccable and angelic glow I'd been admiring about her up to this point was now replaced by the appearance of conjugal shame. She lowered her face and wiggled her ring finger toward me, conceding that she was indeed married. It felt like both an apology and an acceptance of guilt. I shook my head and gave her the kind of body language that relayed my disappointment. I felt foolish spending a good chunk of time getting all in this woman's personal business, but not once did I think to ask about her immediate family or relationship status.

Sherie didn't attempt to explain herself; she only gave me a look that I knew meant she had to go. She turned to open the driver's side door of her convertible Audi S5 then quickly slammed it closed. The car engine started, the gears shifted from park to drive, and the tires screeched. I was left standing there feeling like a damn fool as I watched her brake lights and right turn signal glow in the distance.

Chapter 4

Sherie summoned me to her office first thing Monday morning. I let out a long, frustrated grunt because I was certain that impromptu meeting was to discuss the scandalous ending of last Friday. I was in no mood for an intense exchange this early in the day; however, regardless of the reason, refusing a manager's request probably wouldn't work well in my favor.

Driving home from the restaurant, I talked to my bruised ego, and we agreed that going forward we were not interested in Sherie. We didn't appreciate that she deceived us with her marital status, and she would most certainly be getting the cold shoulder treatment. I held a quick self-coaching session to reinforce this action plan as I made my way to her office. I wouldn't care if I walked in and she was laying naked on her desk. Sherie didn't deserve a drop of compassion from me.

"You wanted to see me?" I was dull and detached.

She went straight to apologizing several times. It wasn't her intention not to talk about her husband, but she got caught up in all my charm. At first, she felt there was nothing inappropriate about being friendly; however, she got too comfortable and allowed herself to accept the spark between us.

"What sucks is that I walked away from a great time with you only to rush home to my good-for-nothing, cheater of a husband."

She turned in her chair to look out the window and began sobbing. I'd only seen Sherie as a woman king. She was forced to possess a rock-solid demeanor as she navigated around our male dominant corporation. Seeing this sensitive side of her caught me off guard. Her vulnerability in this moment was more important than my bruised ego from last weekend.

"I'm sorry that happened to you. I just went through the same thing a couple of months ago." I empathized.

"Ten years of my life wasted." She turned in my direction, expressing disbelief.

"But you're gorgeous, successful, and young enough to move on to a long, loving life with the next man."

"I appreciate you trying to help me look on the bright side, but there's not a chance that love will ever live here again."

"You're hurting right now, it's easy to feel that way. I said the same thing, but it looks to be just a temporary setback," I confessed.

Sherie smiled at my comment, realizing the connection from our meeting last month. She asked why I didn't tell her what I was going through and felt bad to have come down so hard. We shared intimate details about the affairs. The first thing we did after finding out. Both feeling responsible for our cheating partner's indiscretions. Sherie let her transgressor live out of the guest bedroom; I left immediately to allow my ex a few days to move out and haven't spoken to her since.

"I can't afford to leave him right now. There's the mortgage, the credit cards are maxed out, we have two auto loans, and the damn Harley that he never rides is far from paid off. Besides, my daughter would hate me if I kicked her beloved father out of the house."

"So, you're just going to forgive him?"

"No, but I'm not quite sure what to do." I could tell that Sherie felt trapped and annoyed with her predicament.

"You could go to counseling. Makes sense to consider your full situation. I guess couples do tend to stay together for the kids."

The reality of it all must have struck a nerve. Despite me being a newcomer to her personal drama, she let down her guard and was no longer uncomfortable with turning toward the window to hide the tears flowing down her face. I instantly regretted my words and scanned her office for tissues. I could not find any so figured the next best thing would be to offer her a hug. She accepted the embrace; the way she buried her face into my chest felt as if she needed to be held.

We stood there, hugged up, for several minutes. We both got comfortable holding each other – maybe a little too much given the location – but neither of us wanted to be the first to release from the other. I began to slowly circle the middle of her back then switched to applying a massaging pressure.

Sherie let out a light moan. Her breathing increased and warmed my chest. Realizing she approved of my actions, I caressed her back even more then felt her hands move across mine. Her lips kissed my chest; in return, I kissed the top of her head. She raised her face to look in my eyes. We didn't have to say a word. We knew it was time for a kiss.

It was slow and deep and wet, intense and sexy. We each had big, soft lips that from just kissing made our insides tingle and our body parts stand at attention. I could feel her hard nipples on my chest. I was sure she felt my stiff dick poking against her.

Sherie took control of the next moves. She hurried to unbutton my shirt and then hers while we continued to kiss. She grabbed my hand and directed it to her soft, enormous left breast. As I palmed and squeezed her 38 Double-D, she put two of my fingers in her mouth to get them wet and then guided them inside her panties. It was really unnecessary as Sherie's pussy was soaking wet already.

"I want you inside of me," she whispered.

Sherie pulled my necktie, leading me to her desk chair where she forcefully pushed me to sit. Standing in front of me, she began to quickly undress. She unbuttoned her suit blouse and unfastened the front strap of the lace balconette bra she was wearing but left them both on to eliminate wasted time. Her breasts exposed, I pulled her close to me and took in a mouthful of her bosom. They smelled and tasted like cinnamon.

Sherie lifted her skirt and climbed on top of me. The warmth of her pussy excited my body even more. I scooted her satin panties to the left to expose her flesh; she worked her way inside my boxers and fondled my erection before inserting me into her pussy. We moaned in perfect harmony as she slowly bounced on top of me; she felt so good. I feared after just a few strokes, I'd end up disappointing her with a minute man performance.

I cradled her legs and lifted us both from the chair. I wanted to show off and impress Sherie by standing and continuing to give it to her good. She bounced in my arms and we never missed a beat of pleasure nor did my dick slip out from inside her. She covered her mouth to muffle the moans and increased breathing, not wanting her secretary to decipher the noise as sex sounds, while she released what I could tell was a much-needed orgasm.

Sherie begged for me to finish inside her. We didn't consider protection – or the sexual fluids we need to figure out how to clean up after – but we were all-in on loving every minute of this moment and accepting whatever consequences would follow. After I came, Sherie wiped the sweat dripping from my forehead. We smiled at each other and passionately kissed once more before quickly getting dressed.

"Are you able to meet later?" asked Sherie while knotting my tie.

"Round two?"

"No, freak. We need to finish your monthly review."

"And just like that, the bossy, workaholic woman I've known all these years is back." I giggled.

"But just know that after we handle the business, we can jump right back into some more pleasure."

Chapter 5

The unexpected knock on my door put a big smile on my face. I knew it could be no one other than Sherie. My family and friends knew that uninvited guests were absolutely forbidden, but I never mentioned it to Sherie because I felt content with her coming over whenever she wanted. Getting to see her was beginning to be the highlight of my day.

I treasured our special time together despite her relationship status. I didn't mind that I was the side piece, mister, or her emergency dick-in-a-glass. When we were together, Sherie didn't make me feel like I was sleeping with a married woman. She catered to me as if I was the love of her life. True, she was stepping out on her husband to be with me, but from her actions I was convinced that she was my lady.

Sherie was taking greater risks the more connected we became. She visited my place after work almost daily to make love then would leave at a late-night hour unbecoming of a married woman. When we weren't together, she would FaceTime to have phone sex with me while her husband was nearby in the guest bedroom.

No location was off limits. We regularly had sex in her office during my performance review meetings and the backseat of my truck at lunch time in a secluded area of the company parking lot. Once, she gave me a blow job in the back row of a movie theater that we were fortunate to have all to ourselves and yet another while I was driving on the I-10 highway.

"Well, isn't this a pleasant sur–"

I wasn't able to finish with my excitement as I swung the door open to not Sherie as anticipated but rather a strange man. He didn't speak, but his eyes examined me from head to toe several times. Where I came from, staring at another man like that meant a fight was about to go down. I felt disrespected that the unknown brother had the nerve to be challenging me in that way at my own damn doorstep. I sized him up right back and was ready to throw down if needed.

"What's up? Can I help you with something?"

"What you can do is stay away from my wife."

"Man, uh, I think you got the wrong person. I don't know you, so I probably don't know your wife either."

I denied the accusation but knew full well who he was referring to. I knew there would come a day that I'd be standing face-to-face with Darrell, Sherie's husband, I just didn't expect it to be at my front door. How did he find out where I lived? Was it his intention to fight this out or talk this through?

"You don't have to lie about it. I've watched my wife bring her trifling ass over here for the past few months."

"You've been following Sherie?"

"Damn right I've been following her. That's my wife!" He raised his voice.

"I'm not the one you should be hollering at about this. Sherie is a grown woman, and she's told me where y'all stand so choosing to spend time with me is her decision."

"You're right. I will be talking to her later. Right now, I'm standing here talking to you and I'll say it just once – back off and stay away from my wife."

"I get where the hostility is coming from. Finding out that your lady is my lady would be a hard pill to swallow, but you messed up and she chose me."

At this point, I was peeing to mark my turf. It cracked me up how cheaters did what they did and then thought they were in a position to puff their chests out and call shots. Maybe if he came at me humble and unaggressive, I might've been able to empathize with what he was going through. Let's review the situation...

Sherie didn't divorce him for cheating. I saw her only when she wanted to have fun, so obviously, I was just her boy toy. Technically, we were both getting played. However, I wasn't capable of seeing things his way so bowing out gracefully wasn't something I was willing to do. I was in love with Sherie, and I knew she loved me too.

"I'm warning you. Stay away from my wife!" The disgruntled husband shouted.

"Won't be your wife for too much longer, player. Now, step off my porch and don't ever show up at my place again. Won't be this much talking going on if you do."

I slammed my door but peeked out a nearby window, watching his departure. My mind was racing and my blood pressure was boiling. I was also relieved that things did not escalate into a physical altercation. My big and tall stature was outsized by his taller, heavier frame. He was somewhat older so my youth might have been able to jump on him with a few quick one-two combos before he could even get his hands on me, but his advantages were promising his wife to have and hold her until death do us part. Now, that was a connection that was hard to defeat against a man with mixed, angry emotions.

Darrell made the mistake of breaking their vows. Had hoped he could make amends and repair their marriage. Then he found out that revenge was a double-edged sword. It was tough to accept that Sherie was cutting him deeply and killing him slowly by having an affair with me.

I watched as he drove his dark blue Suburban past my window and off the block. My feeling was that this was not the last time that our paths would cross.

Chapter 6

After the exchange with her husband, I insisted that Sherie file for divorce if she wanted to continue seeing me. Her argument was that I knew the situation from the beginning and that she needed more time to improve upon her finances before leaving Darrell could be a consideration. She needed his income to make ends meet and stepping in to take responsibility for the excessive debt that Darrell helped create was not how I envisioned my household life with Sherie to start.

"Wouldn't you get spousal support in the divorce?"

"That bastard won't abide by a damn court order. Besides, with his gambling debt I'm certain he'll always pay late. At least with him being in the house I can expect to get the small amount that he does contribute."

"He cheats on you, has shown you that he is not a good provider, and you're still choosing him over me?"

"I'm not choosing him. I'm choosing my family. I want my daughter to see our stability and teamwork. He may have ruined things with me, but I do not want to interfere with the bond that they have. It's just not a good time to spring this on her."

"I am not going to wait forever for you to leave him." I declared.

"I promise you won't have to."

She held open her arms, closed her eyes, and puckered her lips. I hesitated walking over to oblige her request for affection because for me the conversation was not over; however, I could never deny her my love. She just knew what to say and do to win me over. If I had to, I would wait a hundred years to have her all to myself.

Chapter 7

"Hey, Miles."

I sighed heavily and shook my head before responding to the one person I wished to never speak to again. I made a mental note to stop by Home Depot and purchase a Wyze doorbell camera. That way, I could use the app on my iPhone to see who was there and then choose to ignore the type of unwelcomed visitors I'd had to endure over the past couple of weeks – first Sherie's punk ass husband, Darrell, and now this cheating bitch, Evette.

"Why are you here?"

"Damn, is it like that?"

"It's definitely like that. After what you did, there's no reason you and I ever need to speak again."

As I was about to slam the door shut, Evette told me that she left some important paperwork. Since our breakup, I hadn't made time to scan through the entire apartment for any items she may have left, but if I had discovered anything belonging to her, I would have immediately thrown it away. I knew that was petty, but I was that angry when I found out months back that she had sex with her co-worker while away on a company retreat.

We hadn't spoken since the breakup. She must've called me a hundred times, but I was way too angry to talk. I requested that Verizon disconnect her phone line – after remembering that the account was in my name, and I paid the bill – and eventually I had to change my digits because Evette started calling me from a bunch of random numbers.

Not having a way to make contact with me by phone explained the visit. She knew I despised people just popping up at my place and had to know I hated her for cheating on me, so whatever she left behind must have been seriously needed for her to make the walk of shame back to my doorstep. It was unfair that women got away with bleaching our clothes, keying our cars, and posting cruel things about us on social media, but men were always expected to swallow their pride and be the bigger person.

"Make it quick. The less time I have to be around you, the better the air will be to breathe."

"Wow, you really do hate me."

"I don't like you either, but can you blame me?"

"I'll get my things quickly."

I could tell that my ridicule caused her some pain. Despite what she did, I didn't want to live life with hate in my heart. It wouldn't allow either of us closure and certainly wouldn't help the life connection I intended to have with Sherie. It would control me and stunt my emotional growth, negatively reacting anytime someone new did something that closely resembled how Evette treated me. I did not want my life to be traumatized in that way. I guessed there was no choice but for me to be the bigger person.

"How's everything been with you?" My tone was still a little stank, but my intentions were cordial.

"Okay, I guess. Nothing to brag about but nothing to complain about either."

"All the years I've had no choice but to listen to you gloat about how you are the reason why your company is still in business and now you don't have anything to brag about?" I teased.

"True, I was the best thing that company ever had."

"Was? Had?" I wondered about the nature of her past tense response.

"Yeah, you heard right. I quit my job."

"Why would you do that?"

"It's a long story. Not sure there's enough time to tell you all about it without funking up the place with my odor," Evette said sarcastically.

"Now, I was trying to be cool with you but here you go messing up a happy home. Oops, my bad, you already did that."

"Wow, one point for Miles."

"No way in hell I can catch up to your all-time points total, you being the master asshole and all." I joked.

"Someone is on a roll. It really is a lot involved with why I left; I don't want to wear out my welcome."

"I said it was okay for you to come in, and I asked about work, so if you feel like talking then I'm listening."

"Okay, I'll tell you all about it just as soon as I get this box down."

Evette was struggling to reach a rather large box from the top shelf of my bedroom closet. I was in that closet daily, so I was not sure how I failed to see it given the size. Not only was it big, but it also had some weight to it. I must've helped put it up there at some point because there was no way she lifted the box onto the shelf by herself.

"Shit!" I yelled.

"What happened? Are you okay?"

"I don't know. I felt a pop in my neck when I pulled this damn heavy box toward me."

The box fell to the ground, and I immediately collapsed to the floor, squirming and grabbing my neck from the throbbing pressure and tightness escalating with every second. Evette came down to comfort me. She was touching the painful area to find exactly where I was affected. Once she found the spot that hurt, she lightly massaged my neck. Her hands felt so magical and were definitely helping relieve some of the soreness.

I began to relax and allowed myself to enjoy how wonderful her touches were making me feel. My eyes were closed, I let out some soft moans, and in that moment, my mind totally forgot about the ill feelings I had for Evette fucking another man earlier this year.

"Let's see if you can stand up and make it to the bed. I'm sure I can work out that kink in your neck if you were lying in a better position," said Evette.

The pain was somewhat fading, thanks to the deep tissue massage Evette was giving me. I had to give credit where it was due; she was always good with her hands. They were small but matched her body as she was a petite woman. Being the big-framed man that I was, it always surprised me that a woman her size would be able to dig in deep to work out any muscle aches that I had. When she asked me to relocate from the floor to the bed, I quickly did as I was told, not ready just yet for her hands to stop touching me and making my neck feel better.

I took off my shirt then laid face down on the bed. Still familiar with where I kept things, Evette opened the bottom drawer of my bedside nightstand to pull out the jar of coconut oil I kept there. Rubbing a quarter size portion into my skin, she continued with massaging my neck, shoulders, and back. She spoke to me softly, instructing me to inhale through my nose and exhale through my mouth. It didn't take long for me to fall into a deep level of relaxation, and shortly after that, I fell asleep.

Chapter 8

I was not sure how long I was out or exactly what time it was right now. I didn't keep an alarm clock by my bed, and my iPhone was probably on the recliner chair in the living room. It was daytime – around ten-thirty in the morning – when I hurt my neck, and Evette was gracious enough to give me the massage that put me to sleep. Opening my eyes just now to a dark room made it clear that several hours had passed and it was sometime in the evening.

Awaking and coming more to my senses, I discovered that Evette was asleep near the edge of my California king size bed. Knowing her for all the years that we were together, I smiled to myself, realizing that she stayed because there was no way she was going to leave without first making sure that I was feeling better. I always loved that about her; she treated me in such a caring manner when we were together.

She made sure I ate a home cooked meal every day, would clean the house, washed my clothes, shaved my head, pedicured my feet, and ensured daily that the royal penis received its happy ending. I never requested these acts of kindness from her – they were all just stuff Evette naturally loved to do for her man – and I knew she was genuine about it because she never did those things expecting for me to reciprocate. Her actions made it easy for me to cherish her and give her any and everything she ever wanted or needed from me.

I noticed that my neck didn't have one speck of pain any longer, and I was thankful that Evette hooked me up with a massage. She came here with a purpose that didn't include tending to me; she could've gotten her paperwork and went on her way. Despite how we ended and what Evette did to betray me, I appreciated that she stuck around and felt good about her being the one that was here to care for me.

She was lying in the opposite direction with her back facing me. I scooted in close behind her to spoon and wrap my arm around her. I was surprised that my hand made contact with her bare skin. For a second, I was shocked because how dare she think it was okay to get that comfortable around me given our current status and all. Then, I eased up and I remembered that Evette did not believe in lying down in a bed with clothes on and that she also preferred to sleep in the nude. I'd seen and touched her naked body a million times before today. It felt familiar and brought back fond memories of the loving, romantic times that we once shared.

My touch must've startled Evette; her body jumped as she began to awaken. Realizing it was me and in agreement to the closeness, Evette wiggled her plump backside against my dick. We slowly grinded against each other for several minutes. Then, she did my favorite gesture she knew was a surefire way to get the sex party started. She reached behind to lift up one of her ass cheeks so that my dick could rest comfortably and perfectly between the crack of her ass; like puzzle pieces locking firmly into position with one another. My dick was as stiff as it could be, and I was certain that Evette knew that the hard thing poking in between her ass was happy to be home. We both moaned in agreeableness of how perfect our bodies felt to each other.

"Well, hello there, stranger," Evette softly whispered over her shoulder.

"Thank you for staying."

"How's your neck feeling?"

"It's okay now, thanks to you," I brightly responded.

"It was the least I could do since it's my fault you got hurt in the first place."

"Yeah, it is your fault," I said playfully.

"Is there anything else I can do to make you feel better?"

I moved my hand up her body to fondle her breasts. Evette had small titties, but I adored her large nipples. They stayed hard and protruding, and it was her sex spot. Licking, sucking, and nibbling lightly on them drove her crazy. Evette could reach climax just from me pleasuring her nipples.

What she lacked up top in cup size, she most certainly made up for it down below with her bodacious apple bottom booty. She was a medium-built woman possessing a flat midsection but was bottom heavy with thick thighs. Evette was sexy in clothes and in her birthday suit. When we were together, I never had to look anywhere else for eye candy.

"Now you know damn well that's my spot."

"I know exactly what it is."

"Please Miles, make love to me." Evette requested.

Evette reached around from behind her to take my dick in her hand, sliding me inside her already soaking wet pussy. I didn't waste any time to thrust her with quick, passionate strokes. I did this on purpose, wanting to make sure she felt every inch of what she was missing since our breakup. She panted and thrusted back, talking dirty to me, demanding that I fuck her harder and faster.

It didn't take long for Evette to reach climax – she was nearly there before we started fucking as a result of my nipple foreplay – and it wasn't much longer for her to cum twice more. We switched positions to Evette on top of me, riding me, working her way to orgasm number four. She continued to bounce on my dick until I was the next contestant to have a sexual eruption.

Evette laid on my chest right after we finished. Our breathing was still heavy. Our bodies were both covered in sweat. Her pussy was swollen and full of cum. My hard dick reverted back to being limp and relaxing until the next time I needed the little guy for another fuck session. In that moment, I chose to forget about the scandalous shit Evette did that split us apart and remembered only the reasons why I loved her in the first place.

Chapter 9

I was usually out like a baby but wasn't able to sleep much last night. My mind was too busy wandering with questions and thoughts about the predicament I'd got myself into. The morning sun slapped me with guilt and displeasure because what happened with Evette no longer felt like a satisfying blast from the past. Why did I let us go there? How could I be so weak? What did this all even mean? Where did we go from here?

Evette was not supposed to be in bed with me right now. I certainly enjoyed those forty-five minutes of sex, but just like that, I ruined and disrespected my love connection with Sherie. Then again, Sherie was a married woman and had showed me that she intended to stay that way. I was single and entitled to do whatever I wanted and with whomever I chose. Even still, I couldn't have Evette thinking that last night was make up sex because I was definitely not ready to forgive her for cheating on me.

"Where's the kiss you used to give me before getting out of bed?" Evette said after a long, drawn-out yawn.

"Obviously, a lot has changed."

"Nothing at all has changed about your love making. You are still number one in my book."

"Well, I aim to please."

"Indeed, you did." Evette purred.

"Must not have been that good. I didn't wake up smelling pancakes."

"Well, you just said things have changed," she responded playfully.

"Look at you. One point for Evette."

"On a serious note, I am hoping that last night meant we can work on things going back to how they once were?"

"I'm not sure that would be a good idea right now," I responded with disdain.

"Oh, but it was a good idea to make love to me last night?"

I sighed loudly, wanting her to sense how annoyed I was at her assumption that one night of sex with me exonerated her from destroying a five-year relationship with yet another night of sex that she selfishly had with someone else.

"It was just sex for me," I said bluntly.

"That hurts that you would say that."

"Hurt people hurt people."

"Maybe I should just go," Evette said, displeased with my response.

"That would be best. I'm getting in the shower now. Lock my door when you let yourself out."

Giving the cold shoulder to Evette was the right thing to do. Maybe there would come another time where I could forgive what she had done, but I refused to allow her to think that she could cheat on me and then make it all better with sex. I was just gonna let her feel butt hurt for a while, and if I ever again wanted to have a piece of her, then I'd make contact. It felt really good having the upper hand with this situation.

Chapter 10

Evette stormed out of Miles' bedroom, furious with how he had dismissed her. She'd rather leave the scene in that fashion then apologize for breaking his heart. She was competitive in all aspects of her life so losing or not getting her way boiled her blood pressure. Miles could consider one day being friends again with Evette, but it would have to be on his terms. However, it was too soon, and he did not feel ready just yet to reconcile with her.

Just as she swung open the front door to leave, Sherie was in motion to knock. They stared curiously at each other, a little shocked, and very puzzled as to what business the other had being there. Both internalized that they must be standing in the presence of a current or former girlfriend, yet neither wanted to be the first to reveal to the other the assumed significance they held.

"May I help you?" Evette asked.

"I'm sorry. I must be at the wrong place. I was looking for–"

"Miles."

"Oh, so I am at the right house. Is he here?"

"Who are you?"

"Sherie. Miles and I work together. Who are you?"

"Evette."

"Wait. You're Evette? His ex-girlfriend, Evette?" Sherie asked excitedly and was now very concerned as to what she was doing at Miles' place.

"I see Miles has talked about me. Unfortunately, he's never mentioned you," Evette responded with malicious intent.

"Is he here or not?" Sherie sighed outwardly, disliking where this conversation was headed.

"Was he expecting you? You must be new and not know him very well because Miles doesn't—"

"Like uninvited guests. Yes, I know. I've stopped by to surprise him many times, and I can assure you he has no problem with that when it comes to me." Sherie quipped.

"If that's true, then I guess you must be someone special. He's here but in the shower right now, cleaning up from the wonderful time we had last night." Evette quipped back.

"You know what, bi—"

"Come on in and make yourself at home. I was just about to leave; my work here is done." Evette dismissively cut off Sherie midsentence.

Evette rushed past Sherie, leaving her standing at the entryway, baffled at what had just transpired. Sherie was disturbed by the news that Miles and Evette had sex last night. Here she was coming over to surprise him with takeout food from Mrs. White's Golden Rule Café – the restaurant where they had their first date – wanting to make amends for not being available much lately due to work demands and the complicated situation going on at home with her estranged husband. While Sherie had plans to feed him then fuck him really good, Miles obviously had his own agenda that didn't include her.

Her eyes began to fill with tears. Despite the reality of being married to Darrell and having an affair with Miles, she felt wronged and betrayed by his lack of sensitivity with handling her heart. She thought they were in love. Miles knew in advance that she was married and he went along with it. She was honest with him from the jump; however, he never informed her that he was sleeping with someone else, even more so with Evette.

Her first thought was to angrily call him out on his bullshit and let him know how disappointed she was with his actions, but her better judgment decided against it. Her tears mixed with the mascara she wore flowed down her face and dripped black spots onto her white blouse. Sherie decided right then to remember how this moment made her feel and that she would not allow Miles to cause her pain in this way ever again. If this was the type of treatment she would receive from a man that claimed he loved her, then she might as well stay attached to the infidelity she already had to deal with from Darrell.

Chapter 11

"Please have a seat, Mr. Brandston." Sherie gestured to the chair opposite the desk where she sat.

She had been avoiding me at the office and not taking my calls or returning my texts for a few weeks now, but I had no clue why she was suddenly ghosting me. I made the assumption that she had most likely worked out her marital issues. I figured she would probably never leave Darrell. She made it plainly clear in the beginning, but I also thought she respected and cared for me enough to end things better than with the silent treatment.

"So, it looks like the same way we started is the same way we'll end?" I said with disgust.

"What exactly is that supposed to mean?"

"It's about you and this stiff, corporate, boss lady persona you are giving me right now. Where is the woman I love? The woman I knows loves me back?"

"The only woman I can be to you right now, Mr. Brandston, is the one that you are meeting with about your performance review. Besides being your boss, there's nothing more to discuss."

"I should've known better than to get involved with a married woman," I said under my breath but still loud enough for her to make out what I said.

"Yes, you did know I was married. However, I was never made aware that you were still fucking your ex."

Sherie raised her voice and spoke with attitude and anger when she revealed what I believed to be the reason why she cut me off. How did she know about Evette? Now that I think about it, the same day Evette and I had sex was also about the last time I heard from Sherie. Did their paths cross somehow and I didn't know about it? Or was Sherie stalking my place the same as her husband, Darrell? It made sense they were staying together; their crazy, insecure asses deserved each other.

"Evette means nothing to me!" I declared.

"I must not have meant anything to you either because according to Evette, you never mentioned me."

"Whatever Evette said was obviously to get under your skin. What happened between her and I was a terrible mistake."

"Let me guess. You fell, and your dick just conveniently landed inside of her?" Sherie said with sarcasm.

"Actually, I did fall but not like you are putting it. Besides, I don't have to justify my actions to you as a single man, especially since you are choosing your cheating husband over me."

"I was ready to leave him until I found out about Evette."

"I don't give a damn about Evette, and fuck Darrell too! I choose you, Sherie. Will you choose me?"

I could tell by the overwhelmed look on her face that Sherie was unsure of what to do with my plea. She had never heard me express my love for her in this way. I meant what I said and though there was still so much to figure out I was ready to turn this affair into the real love we both wanted it to be.

"For the sake of my daughter, I can't divorce my husband right now. Plus, I'm your manager, and I've worked too hard to get where I am. I refuse to lose my executive position in this company for sleeping with a subordinate."

If the tables were turned, I'd probably respond the same. Still hurt the heart to hear it. Maybe the silent treatment was the better way to end this. I sat on the other side of her desk, looking away to hide my watery eyes. There was nothing more to be said, so I stood and headed for the door.

"One last thing, Miles."

"Yes, Mrs. Wagner?" I said with an exhausted, uninterested tone.

She smirked at the condescending manner of using her married last name, something I've never done before.

At that moment, I wished that I didn't have to endure this disappointing conversation any further.

"Effective immediately, I will be recommending that you be moved to another team."

"Whatever works for you," I said in defeated agreement.

I continued my exit from her office, content with her decision to subtract me from her life as if I never meant anything to her. If she wanted it like this, then so be it. Probably for the best to get the closure we needed out the way now rather than later. Once I walked out this door, it would be the last time I ever had to deal with her again. I only had myself to blame. I should have left this as the casual sex I initially wanted it to be.

"Are you not going to utilize my golden rule number two?" She hurried to yell out before I left.

I stopped in my tracks to contemplate what Sherie was saying. I turned to face her and could tell right away from studying her eyes that the woman standing in front of me was not my boss at that moment. This was the woman I'd come to love. The woman that, regardless of her current relationship status, I absolutely knew that she was the one for me.

"If at first you don't succeed —"

"Try again until you do." I jumped in to finish reciting Sherie's second rule for success.

I purposely walked at a slow pace back to where Sherie was seated at her desk. I wanted to allow her time to be sure she was content with what our next action would mean. I was walking back to reconcile, to passionately kiss, and maybe for some make up sex too. Most importantly, I was walking back toward Sherie to take what we started and turn it into the greatest thing it could become.

Sherie started to rise from her chair, but I motioned for her to stay seated; she was already in the right position for what I had in mind. I kneeled in front of her, took her hands in mine, and stared into her eyes. I inhaled and exhaled deeply. Pausing for several seconds, I double checked with myself internally to be sure I was content with what I was about to say. I was positive this was what I wanted and was confident that Sherie felt the same. Now was definitely the time we moved forward together.

"It may seem like we have ourselves in a crazy mess, but I'm sure that you and I are capable of making sense of it all."

"Miles, I —"

"Wait just a moment. Please hear me out first."

"Okay, I'm listening." Sherie retreated and gave me the floor to speak.

"I want you to file for divorce. I will try to be patient and understanding of the whole process. Once all of this current stuff is finalized, and in the past, will you do me the honor of being my wife?"

"Absolutely, but the honor will be all mine!" Sherie excitedly responded without hesitation to promise me her hand in marriage.

We gazed at each other and were filled with joy at the direction we just agreed to take our relationship. I rose from bended knee to tightly embrace my bride-to-be. I kissed her passionately for countless minutes while we repeatedly muttered our love for each other. Our breathing intensified as we seductively touched each other while rushing to undress for a lovemaking session in her office.

"I love you, Miles. I will do everything necessary for us to get married as quickly as possible." Sherie declared.

"Over my dead body!" yelled a man's voice.

Sherie and I were so focused on each other that we didn't hear or see the office door open, nor did we know just how long Darrell had been standing there. He held flowers in his hand and had a faceful of tears coming from his eyes. How devastating it must be to see his wife in a position to sexually please another man, and even more unpleasant to hear her declare that she planned on divorcing him to marry me.

I jumped up quickly, attempting to put my clothes back on. Darrell rushed toward me, striking me in the jaw with one heavy hitting blow. I instantly felt weak then fell backwards and crashed my head into the desk. The impact knocked me unconscious as I collapsed to the floor.

Chapter 12

"I warned you to stay away from my wife, motherfucker!"

Just as Darrell was about to hit me again, I woke up, panic-stricken and drenched in sweat. I was relieved to be waking from that nightmare and to not actually be getting another hard blow to my face. From what I recalled receiving from Darrell earlier in Sherie's office, I hoped to never again endure that type of pain. I'd be the first to admit that the beatdown he gave me was rightfully deserved for playing my part in the extramarital relationship I got caught up in with his estranged wife.

"Nurse, he's waking up!"

"Is that you, Cleon?"

"How are you feeling, bro?"

I tried sitting up in the bed but was instantly overcome with dizziness. I scanned the room, realizing that I was in a hospital with tubes running from my nose and beeping machines next to my bedside. Darrell must've really done a number on me. I'd never been in a fight where I got my ass whooped so bad that I was sent to the hospital. I definitely owed him some payback for this; although, now that I was with Sherie there was probably nothing more that needed to be said or done.

"Can you fully hear and see me, Mr. Brandston?" said the nurse while checking my vitals.

"Yes, I'm fine. Can you tell me how I got here?"

"All I know is that you were brought into the emergency room unresponsive with a cerebral contusion, but I'm sure once the detective returns, he can fill in the gaps for you."

"Detective?" I wondered.

"Yeah, homie, one-time was here earlier asking me all these questions about the punk motherfucker that clocked you. I didn't tell him a damn thing because best believe the hood taking care of this shit for you," said Cleon.

"I don't think that is the kind of nonsense talk that he needs to hear right about now," the nurse responded sternly, annoyed with Cleon's ploy for revenge.

"Now that I know my brother is all good, this is most definitely the time to talk about it."

"Where's Sherie?"

"Well, homie–" Cleon was interrupted by a harsh knock on the door that was only capable of being produced by an officer of the law.

"Hello, Mr. Brandston. Nurse, is this a good time to speak with him?"

"Maybe you should ask him if he wants to holler at you right now," snapped Cleon.

"Yes, I am finished checking on him. Mr. Brandston, please buzz me if you need anything. The doctor will be in to speak with you as soon as she can. If you don't mind, I think it's best that your friend comes with me while you discuss things with the detective."

"Nah, I'm staying right here. I'm family and whatever he needs to say to my boy can be said in front of me."

"Cleon, it's cool. How about you head over to my place and bring me back some clothes?"

"I don't know if it's best for you to be here alone, giving a statement without a witness or a lawyer."

"Lawyer? Why would I need a lawyer?" I inquired, probing Cleon for an explanation.

"There's no reason for a lawyer to be involved in this matter. I came here to check on your well-being and talk briefly with you about what occurred," said the smooth-talking detective, assuring me that his presence was friendly and of concern.

"Alright, but I'll be back as soon as I can," Cleon said as he exited the hospital room.

"Your friend's quite a character. Not too trusting of the police, huh?"

"Fair to say all Black people have a legitimate reason to be on guard with those in your profession," I responded plainly and definitively.

"Touché. Well, I don't want to take up too much of your time. I am so relieved that you were able to make a recovery from the horrible thing that happened to you. I'll get to why I am here so that you can rest and recuperate some more. My name is Bill Peters, lead homicide detective with Chandler Police Department."

"Say what?" I quickly adjusted my posture to sit up more in bed, eager to find out why I was being visited by a homicide detective.

"Can you tell me what happened and why Darrell Wagner attacked you?"

I provided Detective Peters with my recollection of what transpired earlier today. Admitted to the affair I was having with Sherie and our plans to marry once she finalized her divorce. Explained I was not proud of the role that I played, and that I was not looking to press charges against Darrell because I could understand where his rage was coming from. Had the tables been turned, I might've done a lot more damage than just punch him out.

"Would you have any idea where Darrell might have gone?"

"I don't know. That asshole is the last person I'm thinking about right now. All I care about is Sherie. Where is she?"

Detective Peters took a moment to breathe and to calm his facial expression. He must have remembered then that I had just awakened unbeknownst of the sickening turn of events that took place between Sherie, Darrell, and myself. In a procedural and investigative tone, and with as much sensitivity as he could muster, the detective reported on what details were known and speculated on what events took place.

After Darrell knocked me unconscious, he next attacked Sherie. Her administrative assistant, Olivia, provided the detective with an eyewitness statement that it was approximately 4:47 p.m. when she entered the office to check on the commotion she heard. She was easily able to identify that it was Darrell hovering over Sherie because she recognized him from so many visits to the office throughout the years. When Olivia screamed, it forced Darrell to remove his hands from around Sherie's neck, then he turned and bolted out the door.

Surveillance cameras were able to record Darrell fleeing from the scene in a dark colored Chevy Suburban, license plate 3-Alpha-7-1-Charlie-7. Officers were not able to apprehend him at the home, but there appeared to be clothes, jewelry, and other valuables removed. His whereabouts were unknown, but a statewide A.P.B. had been initiated in hopes to arrest him as quickly as possible.

"That motherfucker killed Sherie?"

I could hear the heart monitor beep louder and steadier, indicating that my pulse and blood pressure were rising. I let out a cry of anguish. My heart was broken. My soul was consumed with guilt. I instantly felt that what happened to Sherie was all my fault. She wanted to end things with me numerous times before today, but selfishly, I wouldn't allow her.

The detective continued to speak, but I was in shock and so devastated that I heard nothing he said. His last declaration was that his department would do everything it could to catch the perpetrator and hold him accountable for the awful crime that was committed. They had better find him before I did because nothing would stop me from making him pay with his life for what he did to my beloved Sherie.

Epilogue

The barbershop was deathly silent at the conclusion of me telling them everything about what had gone down with me and Sherie. I looked around and could sense different emotions in their eyes. I was the blame to some, the victim to others. Whatever emotion they had at that moment, not one person judged me for what happened. I felt safe and comforted and amongst family who had my back when I was done wrong, but who also put me in my place when the wrongdoing was on me.

"What's your plans now that your job will most likely fire you?" inquired Darius.

"How'd you know about that?"

In unison, everyone pointed in the direction of Cleon, then we all burst into laughter. This was our way of making fun of the reality that when it came to knowing someone's personal business, the undeniable gossiping source would always be him. I wasn't even upset about the intrusion. It was a great way to lighten the mood and get us back to the good vibration we always felt at Goodfellas Barbershop. The hooting and hollering gave me a moment to think to myself about my current employment situation.

After discharging from the hospital, I listened to a voicemail from Human Resources advising me that I was placed on a paid leave of absence. Apparently, this was to allow me time for bereavement, and also until a full investigation of the incident could be completed. With all of the negative media coverage the company endured, I didn't sense this so-called investigation working in my favor, especially since no one from H.R. asked to speak with me to hear my side of the story.

My thinking was that the verdict was already determined. The paid leave was just a public relations ploy to show that I'd been allowed some time to recover from the devastating event. Once things cooled down, I was sure I would next be fired. To be honest, I don't think I could go back to working there. My colleagues and upper management would probably view me differently. Would whisper about me behind my back. Would wonder if my years as the top sales guy under Sherie's leadership was all to me sleeping with the boss.

I doubted I could have the same high level of performance. I couldn't see myself being able to visit that building every workday without languishing over Sherie's passing. Too many memories of her were there. I smelled her perfume, tasted her loins, and asked her to marry me. I would forever mourn my former boss and lover, and couldn't possibly go back to business as usual in that place. I would always feel terrible about what happened to Sherie and regret that I ever crossed the line dating a married woman. The end definitely didn't justify the means.

Right then I decided that, whether or not the investigation cleared my name of responsibility, I would resign at the end of my leave of absence. I promised myself that at the next job I would strictly focus on work. Never again would I get involved with a woman at my place of business.

"I don't know what's next. No clue at all," I responded pitifully.

"I know some work available. Big guy such as yourself would be perfect for the job," said the gentleman getting his beard lined up by Darius.

I took a deep breath and walked over to learn more about the potential employment opportunity. With every step forward, a small piece of the past faded behind me. That was not to say that I would ever be able to forget about Sherie and all the trouble I caused her. May she rest in peace. I just hoped that I learned from this mistake, and that what didn't kill me was meant to make me stronger.

TO BE CONTINUED

DID YOU ENJOY READING THIS BOOK?

Please help others enjoy it, too.

Lend it.
Recommend it.
Review it.

Message me so that I can personally thank you.

www.andrebriscoe.com